I made this
book for:

_____

Love,

Alona

I Want My Mother

I Want

HarperFestival®
A Division of HarperCollinsPublishers

My Mother

Written and illustrated by Alona Frankel

Library of Congress catalog card number: 99-63976
HarperCollins®, ☷®, and HarperFestival® are registered trademarks of HarperCollins Publishers Inc. http://www.harperchildrens.com
"Joshua" is a registered trademark of Alona Frankel. Alona photo: Dina Guna. www.alonafrankel.com

Motto:
Mommy, Mommy, come sit near
Don't leave me alone
'Til I'm big and grown.

Leah Naor

Hello.
My name is Joshua.
I am a boy.
I am a sad boy.
My mother went away.
I want my mother.

My mother is loyal.
My mother is protective.
My mother is warm.
My mother is brave.
My mother is hardworking.
My mother is quick.
My mother is soft.
My mother is funny.
My mother is elegant.
My mother is big and round.
I love my mother.
Mother, come back to me!

"Knock, knock."
"Who's there?"
"Hello! I am a mother.
I am a loyal mother."

"That's right. You ARE a mother.
You ARE a loyal mother.
You are a dog.
You are a puppy's mother.
I want MY mother."

"Knock, knock."
"Who's there?"
"Hello!
I am a mother.
I am a protective mother."

"That's right. You ARE a mother.
You ARE a protective mother.
You are a kangaroo.
You are a baby kangaroo's mother.
I want MY mother."

"Knock, knock."
"Who's there?"
"Hello! I am a mother.
I am a warm mother."

"That's right. You ARE a mother.
You ARE a warm mother.
You are a bear.
You are a bear cub's mother.
I want MY mother."

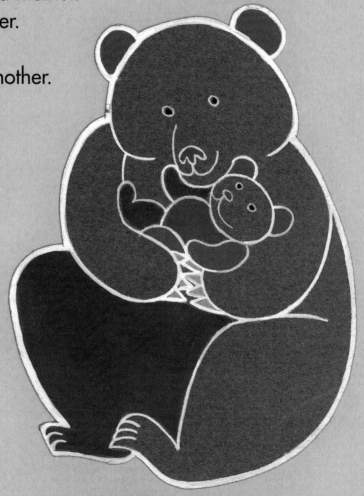

"Knock, knock."
"Who's there?"
"Hello! I am a mother.
I am a brave mother."

"That's right. You ARE a mother.
You ARE a brave mother.
You are a lioness.
You are a lion cub's mother.
I want MY mother."

"Knock, knock."
"Who's there?"
"Hello! I am a mother.
I am a hardworking mother."

"That's right. You ARE a mother.
You ARE a hardworking mother.
You are a squirrel.
You are a little squirrel's mother.
I want MY mother."

"Knock, knock."
"Who's there?"
"Hello! I am a mother.
I am a quick mother."

"That's right. You ARE a mother.
You ARE a quick mother.
You are a deer.
You are a fawn's mother.
I want MY mother."

"Knock, knock."
"Who's there?"
"Hello! I am a mother.
I am a soft mother."

"That's right. You ARE a mother.
You ARE a soft mother.
You are a sheep.
You are a lamb's mother.
I want MY mother."

"Knock, knock."
"Who's there?"
"Hello! I am a mother.
I am a funny mother."

"That's right. You ARE a mother.
You ARE a funny mother.
You are a monkey.
You are a baby monkey's mother.
I want MY mother."

"Knock, knock."
"Who's there?"
"Hello! I am a mother.
 I am an elegant mother."

"That's right. You ARE a mother.
You ARE an elegant mother.
You are a cat.
You are a kitten's mother.
I want MY mother."

"Knock, knock."
"Who's there?"
"Hello! I am a mother.
I am a mother who is
big and round."

"That's right. You ARE a mother.
You ARE a mother who is big and round.
You are an elephant.
You are a baby elephant's mother.
I want MY mother."

"Knock, knock."
"Who's there?"
"Hello!
I am a mother.
I am a loyal mother.
I am a protective mother.
I am a warm mother.
I am a brave mother.
I am a hardworking mother.
I am a quick mother.
I am a soft mother.
I am a funny mother.
I am an elegant mother.
I am a mother who is big and round."

"That's right!
You ARE a mother.
You are MY mother!"

Alona Frankel is the
author and illustrator of
over thirty titles for children,
including the well-known ONCE
UPON A POTTY. She is the recipient
of numerous awards, and her books
and art are seen all around the world.
Ms. Frankel lives in Tel Aviv, Israel.

Find out more about Alona
Frankel on the internet at:
www.alonafrankel.com